ERNST

Elisa Kleven

TRICYCLE PRESS
Berkeley • Toronto

Tricycle Press
a little division of Ten Speed Press
P.O. Box 7123
Berkeley, California 94707
www.triciclepress.com

Interior design: Barbara Powderly
Cover design: Barbara Powderly and Larissa Pickens

The Library of Congress has catalogued an earlier edition
as follows:
Kleven, Elise.
   Ernst / by Elisa Kleven.—1st ed.
      p.   cm.
   Summary: A young crocodile with a vivid imagination
celebrates a birthdray.
   ISBN 0-525-44515-3
   [1. Birthdays-Fiction. 2. Crocodiles-Fiction.] I. Title.
PZ7.K6783875Er   1989   89-1634
[E]-dc19   CIP
                                                 AC

First published in hardcover by Dutton Children's Books, 1989
First Tricycle Press printing, 2002
ISBN-13: 978-1-58246-053-6
ISBN-10: 1-58246-053-1

Printed in China

2 3 4 5 6 — 10 09 08 07 06

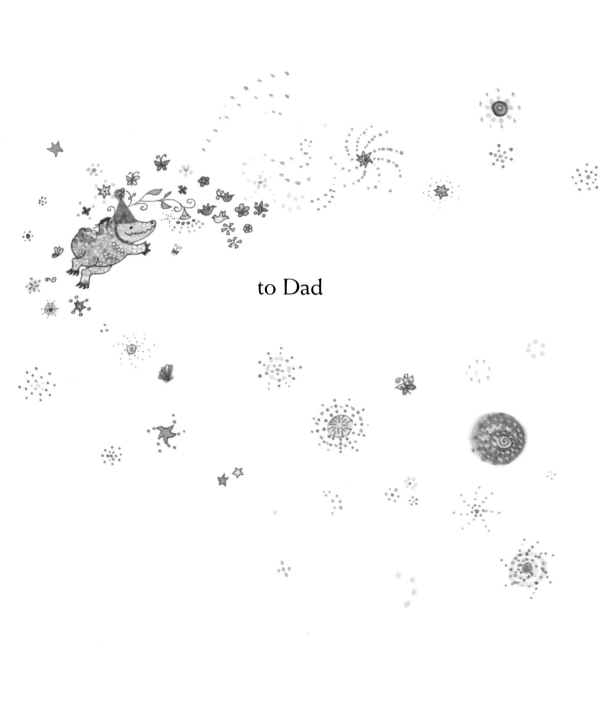

to Dad

Once upon a time, in a world full of light,
trees, bugs, seashells, birds...

and night, there lived a young crocodile named Ernst, who loved to think "What if?"

"What if sand were fudgy instead of sandy?" he'd think when he dug damp holes at the beach.

"What if every-one traveled in magic carts?" he'd think on the hot bike ride home.

"What if grandmas were young?" he'd
think when he sat on his grandmother's soft,
wrinkled lap.

"What if trees never dropped their leaves?" he'd think when he painted the tree outside his window.

"What if the honking school bus could sing?" he wished one day as he trudged off to meet it.

"What if the stars were big?" he asked his mother that starry night as she scurried around the kitchen.

"The stars *are* big," said his mother.

"How big?" asked Ernst.

"Big," said his mother, rolling out the crust for double fudge pie. "Big as worlds. Please get the chocolate and sugar from the pantry, sweetie."

"Mother," said Ernst, as he got the chocolate and sugar. "What if fudge were black-and-white striped, like a zebra?"

"Please call Father down for supper," his mother replied.

"Mother," said Ernst, when he'd called his father. "What if Father were called Pumpernickel instead of Father?"

"Wash up for supper now, Ernst," said his mother.

"Mother and Father," said Ernst at supper. "What if I were a little yellow bird who lived all alone on the moon?"

"If you were a bird like that, then it would be hard for you to eat your dessert," said his mother, handing Ernst a serving of jiggling green Jell-O.

"Mother," said Ernst, as he nibbled his Jell-O. "Why aren't we having double fudge pie for dessert tonight?"

"You know why," said his mother. "Now what if you finished dessert, brushed your teeth, and got into bed?"

"Mother," said Ernst as his mother tucked him in. "What if my birthday came every day?"

"Then it wouldn't be special," said his mother. "Now go to sleep, because tomorrow *is* your birthday."

"I know!" said Ernst, and shut his eyes and thought, w h a t

if .

.

.

he got a spaceship for his birthday,
and blasted off, zooming deep into
the dark, sparkling sky, past zillions
of swirling stars, whirling suns,
comets . . .

past meteors, asteroids, galaxies, and
moons, until he reached a faraway
world . . .

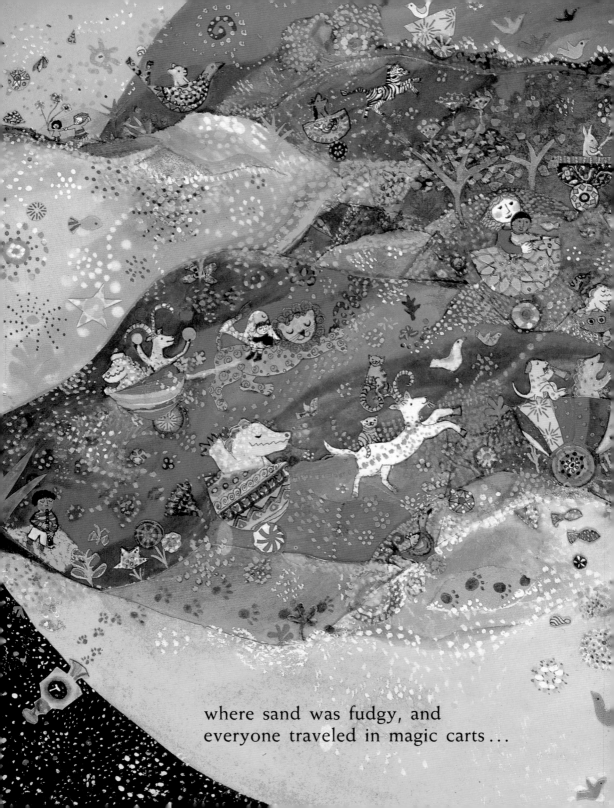

where sand was fudgy, and
everyone traveled in magic carts ...

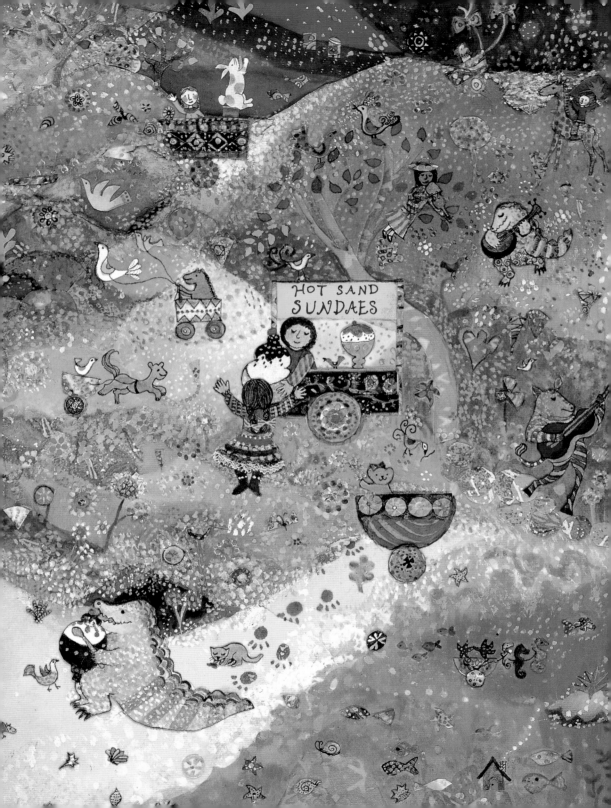

and grandmas were
smooth as ladybugs (and fit
in the palm of your hand),

and trees held on to their leaves
all winter, and the stars above
were no bigger than seashells...

and fudge looked like zebras,

and fathers were
called bagels,

and mothers answered
every question you
asked them. It was a
strange and beautiful
world.

Back in Ernst's own world it was morning, and Mother, Father, and Grandma were waiting with presents and sparkling hats...

and instead of oatmeal for breakfast there was
double fudge pie,

and on the way to school the whole bus sang
"Happy Birthday, dear Ernst!"

Ernst couldn't think of a better world.